TALES FOR TOMÁS

100 Years of Las Vegas

A Tomás the Tortoise Adventure

Mike Miller

For Barbara

For more Tomás adventures visit www.tomasthetortoise.com
Copyright 2004, Mike Miller and Stephens Press LLC

Written and illustrated by Mike Miller
Edited by Laura Brundige

ISBN# 1932173374

CIP Data Available

A *Las Vegas Review-Journal* Book

A Stephens Media Group Company
Post Office Box 1600
Las Vegas, Nevada 89125-1600

Printed in Hong Kong

It All Started About A Hundred Years Ago. . .

Grandpa looked at Tomás and rocked for awhile;
Then he leaned forward to point with a smile:
"Tomás, it is time. I'm a hundred years old.
I know some true stories you've never been told.
You, my dear boy, are almost 23!
It's high time you carried them on, don't you see?"
Tomás the Tortoise was proud and excited;
Grandpa seldom spoke, but now he'd invited
Young Tomás to listen and learn at his side!
Tomás settled down quickly, eyes and ears open wide.

First were The Meadows, a place down below
Where my Grammy and Grampy lived, long, long ago
Before this old desert, dry and windblown
Became the Las Vegas that's so very well known.

The neighbors were Paiutes — good neighbors, too —
Who never took more from the land than their due.
They moved with the seasons, to harvest the seeds,
And the desert and mountains met all of their needs.

But one day Grampy was startled to see Spaniards riding
On beasts with long legs that sent him into hiding!
He watched as they traveled far, far to the west
And picked out a path where the footing was best.

More followed, and more, on the Old Spanish Trail.
They carried fine woolens, and money, and mail
From far Santa Fe to the towns on the coast,
To trade for whatever they needed the most.

Great herds of strong horses and mules thundered past,
And stopped at The Meadows to graze on the grass.

They were followed by soldiers, mapping the path. Explorer John Fremont stopped here for a bath.

And then came the Mormons, using the route
To link Salt Lake City with ports to the south.
They built forts and towns along the whole way;
And those became cities that remain 'til today!

The miners came, too. At first they found lead
At Potosi Mountain, but Grandpappy said
They couldn't make bullets from the bright, heavy stuff.
Then others found silver, and gold! Quite enough!

And borax! And gypsum! And I don't know what else.
It made people dream of bringing that wealth
On chugging steam trains along straight iron rails
That carried rich cargo up the Old Spanish Trail.

Those trains needed water darn near every hour
To turn into the steam that gave them their power.
Big Springs, at The Meadows, was the logical source.
The rails were laid out right by there, of course.

So people who saw a bright future a-coming
Moved to The Meadows and set things a-humming,
Diverting its stream to water new farms
And planting their crops with hard work and strong arms,
Awaiting the railroad. They bet it would be
The pride of the West in the new century!

Amid this excitement, in nineteen-ought-three,
A tortoise hatched out. That youngster was me!

The bustle was more than my parents could stand.
We moved farther west, to a quieter land
Where mountains, and canyons, and big red rocks there
Sheltered us all from the dust in the air.

The eager new settlers built with canvas and pine,
Still awaiting the coming of trains down the line.
And the trains finally got here in 1905.
A land auction made a new town come alive!

We still raised our families.
Still the town grew.
We learned we could live
  with whatever was new.
Those people had energy!
  Couldn't sit still!
We watched it all happening
  from Calico Hill.

We'd barely grown used to the wagons and horses
When we had to contend with unnatural forces.
Autos and trucks ran on smoke, smell, and noise!
We hid in our burrows like scared little boys.

In distant Los Angeles the future looked bright:
Electricity would come to light up the night
From the wild Colorado, an untamed red river.
Once they dammed it, they'd generate power forever!

A dam would stop floods that drowned valleys below;
Instead, they'd be saved up and steadily flow
To green valleys that formed all America's farm;
It would turn to good purpose the old source for harm.

Six years it took,
  from first shovel and hoe,
To tame the great river
  and send water below.
It took workers by thousands,
  from 48 states.
Some stayed in Nevada,
  and live here to this date!

A world war was brewing in Poland and Spain;
We'd won such a war, and could do it again!
An air base was built here, and factories, too!
Some people lost sons, for patriots do.

Peace was not certain,
  those following years.
Folks wanted big weapons
  to quiet their fears.
At a barren desert site
  not too far away,
Testing the bombs
  turned the night into day.

But then the war ended,
  and people soon found
Time to travel and visit
  our desert playground.
Las Vegas spread south
  on a strip through the sand.
We sprouted an airport,
  and jets came to land.
High-rise casinos sprang up
  like huge blocks,
Built by huge cranes and
  tractors that scared off my socks!

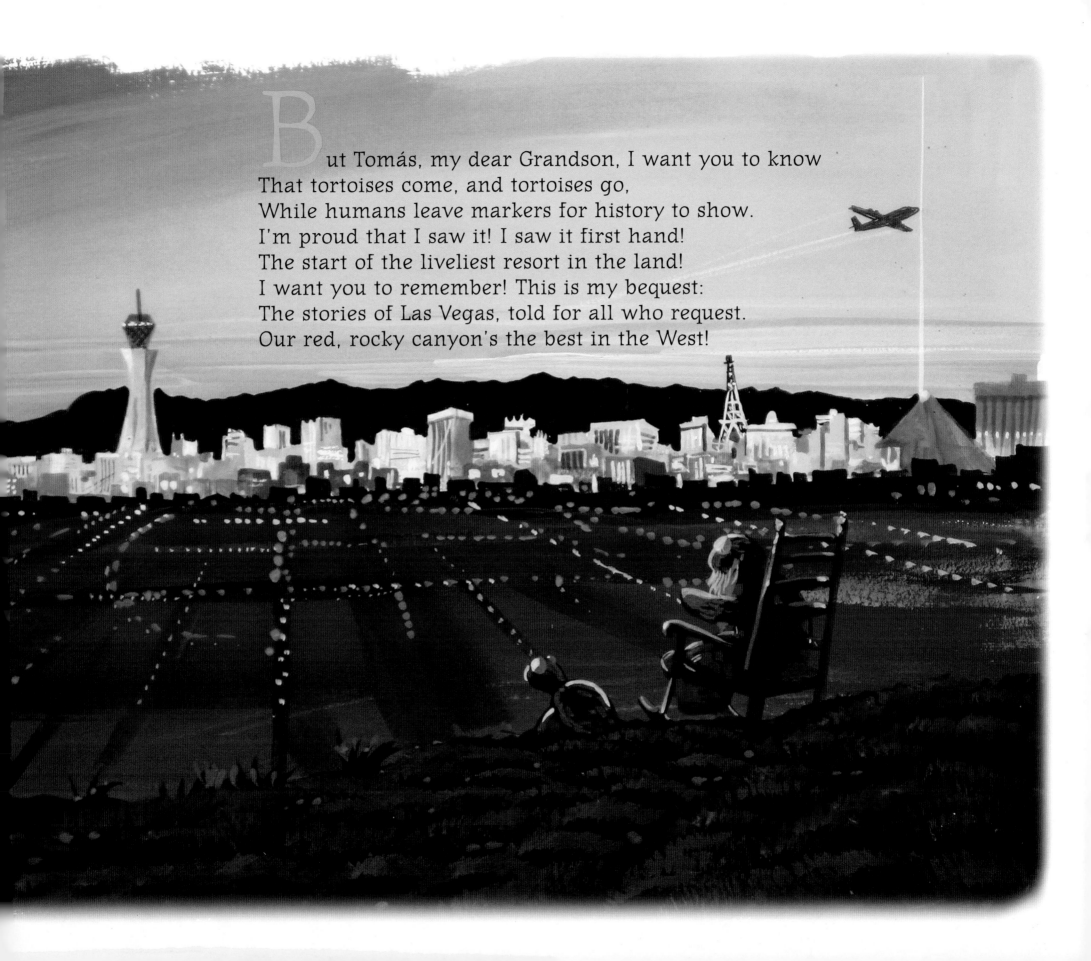

But Tomás, my dear Grandson, I want you to know
That tortoises come, and tortoises go,
While humans leave markers for history to show.
I'm proud that I saw it! I saw it first hand!
The start of the liveliest resort in the land!
I want you to remember! This is my bequest:
The stories of Las Vegas, told for all who request.
Our red, rocky canyon's the best in the West!

LAS VEGAS: THE BIRTH OF A CITY

1830   First Mexican trading caravan from New Mexico stops at Las Vegas Springs en route to Pacific Coast

1844   John C. Fremont heads U.S. Army troop into Las Vegas Valley to refresh at Las Vegas Springs

1852   Mail route established from Salt Lake City through Las Vegas Valley to Pacific Coast

1855   Mormon settlers establish mission in Las Vegas Valley from Salt Lake City to San Bernardino, California

1855-1858   Mormons build Fort and divert Las Vegas Spring water for farming and irrigation

1865   Octavius Gass takes over abandoned fort and starts the Las Vegas Ranch, which expands into major agricultural center

1900   Construction begins on railroad from Salt Lake City to Los Angeles

1905   Las Vegas City established; first train arrives by rail; land auction begins

1909   Las Vegas becomes County Seat of newly established Clark County

1930   Construction begins on Hoover Dam

1931   Gambling legalized in Las Vegas

1935   Completion of Hoover Dam

1940-1947   U.S. Army Aerial Gunnery School trains fliers and bombers north of Las Vegas

1942   Basic Magnesium plant opens in Henderson to aid in war effort

1949   U.S. Air Force establishes Nellis Air Force Base at Gunnery School site

1940-1950   First resort hotels open south of Las Vegas on old Los Angeles Highway

1950-1960   Growth on Los Angeles Highway blossoms into the start of the Las Vegas Strip

1951   Atomic testing begins at the Nevada Test Site

1960-1980   Las Vegas Valley growth of tourism and resort hotels establishes Las Vegas as "The Entertainment Center of the World"

1980-2005   Population grows to over 1,400,000. Now Las Vegas has 9 of the 10 largest resort hotels in the world and has become truly an international destination.